This book belongs to

_____

Walt Disney® VOLUME 4
BIG AND LITTLE, SAME AND DIFFERENT

WALT DISNEY FUN-TO-LEARN LIBRARY

®

A BANTAM BOOK
NEW YORK · TORONTO · LONDON · SYDNEY · AUCKLAND

ISBN 0-553-05504-6

Published simultaneously in the United States and Canada. Bantam Books are published by Bantam Books, a division of Bantam Doubleday Dell Publishing Group, Inc. Its trademark, consisting of the words "Bantam Books" and the portrayal of a rooster, is Registered in U.S. Patent and Trademark Office and in other countries. Marca Registrada. Bantam Books, Inc., 1540 Broadway, New York, New York 10036. Printed in the United States of America.
19 18 17 16 15   Classic® binding, R. R. Donnelley & Sons Company. U.S. Patent
No. 4,408,780; Patented in Canada 1984; Patents in other
countries issued or pending.

"I love to fly!" shouts Peter Pan. "Flying is the best fun there is!"

Peter is on his way to visit Wendy and John and Michael Darling. Can you help him find the way?

Peter watches for four towers. Three are just the *same*. One is *different*. He knows he must turn when he sees the different one. Will you show him where it is?

On his way Peter had to fly over a park. He knew he had to fly towards one tree that was different from the others. Can you see the different tree?

"I see Wendy's house!" Peter exclaims. "It looks different from the others." Do you see it, too?

Upstairs in the nursery Wendy, John, and little Michael are busy playing. "Here's how I build a tower," Michael tells Wendy. Can you see the towers that are shaped the same?

"Look at the Indians in my picture," says John proudly. Can you find the Indians that are just the same?

Now John and Michael want to play pirates. John waves his *long* wooden sword. "Clear the decks," he shouts. Michael's sword is *shorter*. The boys knock down Michael's block towers and bump into everything. See what they've done to the nursery!

"Look out!" says Wendy. The *big* rocking chair almost falls over. Nana the dog catches it — just in time.

Do you see a *smaller* chair in the picture? Guess who will sit in it when the sword fight is over.

"Peter is here!" Wendy runs to
the window to welcome her friend.
Naughty Tinker Bell makes a
face at Wendy. "I'm Peter's friend,"
she thinks.

John and Michael can't wait for their Never Land adventure to begin.

Do you see the three beds in the nursery? John has the *longest* bed. Whose bed is *middle-sized*? And who has the *shortest* bed of all?

Most of the toys have been put away. But John and Michael forgot the toy boats lying on the floor. The *biggest* boat looks like a pirate ship. That belongs to John. The *smallest* is a rowboat. That is Michael's favorite. Do you see a *middle-sized* boat, too?

Tinker Bell and Peter fly all around the nursery. "Look how well I fly!" shouts Peter. Tinker Bell thinks, "I'm even better than Peter. He can't somersault through the air like I can."

Is Tinker Bell bigger than Peter? Or is she smaller? Can you tell?

Soon Peter and Tinker Bell will teach Wendy and her brothers how to fly.

Nana and the teddy bear are watching. Maybe they would like to fly, too. Which one is bigger?

As the children are flying around the nursery, in far-off
Never Land, the pirates watch for Peter to come back. One of
the pirates looks different from the others. Can you find the
different one? Why does he look so frightened?

The Indian chief and his friend want to catch fish for their dinner. The *shorter* Indian has hooked something very big. Do you think he can hang onto his pole? Maybe the chief, who is *taller*, will help him.

Look at the fine fish lying on the shore. Which fish is longer?

"Today we hunt. Follow me," says the big chief. He is the *tallest* Indian. Find the *shortest* Indian. Do you see a *middle-sized* Indian, too?

Three totem poles guard the Indian village. Which one is the tallest? Which is shortest? And is there a middle-sized pole, too?

"A fierce animal is coming!" The shortest Indian has climbed up on a stump so that he can look around.

"Run," he shouts. "Run away!"

The tall chief and his friend look for places where they can hide. A tall tree will make a good hiding place for the chief. Help him find one. Find a tree that is just right for the shorter Indian, too.

What do you think frightened the Indians? Maybe those friendly rabbits can tell us.

While the Indians hide, the pirate ship bounces over the waves.

"I'm hungry!" roars fierce Captain Hook. He cuts a *thick* slice of pirate-food cake for his lunch. "I'm hungry, too," says Smee in a soft voice. But Captain Hook doesn't listen. He cuts a *thin* slice for First Mate Smee.

The other pirates are still waiting for their cake. "We'd like thick pieces, too," they say. They have found boards to sit on while they eat their lunch. But what is happening to the thin board? Do you think the thick board will break?

Now Peter and the Darlings are in Never Land. "Flying is easy," Peter says. "Look at me!" He whizzes *over* the top of an old hollow tree. But Wendy is still learning to fly. She wobbles as she flies *under* a branch.

"*Whoooo!*" cries the sleepy owl. "What noisy person woke me up?"

Up, up John goes into the air. And *down*, down comes Michael. The big bear is surprised when he sees a teddy bear coming down from the sky.

"*Grrr*," he growls. "It's raining boys and bears!"

Peter wants to show his friends all of Never Land. He flies *in front of* Wendy to lead the way. Tinker Bell comes along *behind* and watches out for danger.

"Look down there," Peter shouts. "Captain Hook is in trouble." The captain splashes along just in front of the hungry crocodile.

"I'll save you, Captain!" shouts Smee. He is behind the crocodile, and he rows hard to catch up.

"We'd better not get too close to the pirate ship," Wendy says. She sees pirates in the crow's nest near the *top* of the mast, and more pirates at the *bottom*. One pirate has climbed to the *middle* of the mast. He's shouting at Peter! But Peter isn't scared of anything. He swoops in to cut the sails. Once the sails are gone, the boat will stop moving.

In the underground house under Hangman's Tree, Tinker Bell signals a warning. The pirates are coming to seek their revenge! The boys hurry to the ladder. They are all ready to fight the pirates.

Who is at the top of the ladder? Who is on the bottom?

Tinker Bell flies up over a stool where she can see what's happening. Who hides under the stool, hoping the pirates won't find him?

"Ahoy, you pirates!" shouts Peter. "Watch out for me!"
Up he flies, up from the door of the underground house.
The pirates are afraid. "Help!" shouts one.
"Save me!" shouts another.
"Great skulls and crossbones," says a third. "Let's hide."
They all jump down from Hangman's Tree and run away.

Oh-oh. While Peter chases the pirate crew, wicked Captain Hook has captured Tinker Bell. He takes her back to the ship and puts her *inside* a lantern to keep her prisoner.

Tinker Bell is very angry. She kicks the glass and shakes her fist at Hook. Hook just laughs, but Smee is afraid. He's glad he's *outside* the lantern and Tinker Bell is inside where she can't reach him.

"When the Lost Boys come to rescue Tinker Bell,
I'll capture them, too," roars Hook. "I'll lock them up
and never let them out," he promises.

Hook leaves the lantern *on top of* the table. Poor
Smee! He shivers and shakes when the captain is
angry. He hides *under* the table.

Don't worry, Tinker Bell. The Lost Boys are on their way. "We'll find Tinker Bell," John says bravely. He is in front, leading the search party. Who is behind all the others and trying hard to keep up?

Look! Four of the pirates are hiding along the way. They want to know where the Lost Boys are going. The first pirate hides inside something. The second hides behind something. Do you see the third pirate on top of that rock? Where is the last pirate hiding?

Do you know where Peter is? He's off to find the ship—and Captain Hook.

"Follow me!" John orders. "Forward, march."
He marches right under a waterfall. John's umbrella
keeps him *dry*, but poor Michael gets all *wet*.
Is the teddy bear wet, or is he dry?

"Step on the rocks to cross the river," Cubby says. But one rock turns out to be a hippopotamus! Cubby slips off into the water. Now who is wet? Who is dry?

At last the Lost Boys reach the pirate ship and Peter zooms down from the sky.

"Away you go, Captain Hook," shouts Peter. He pushes the captain right off the rigging. Smack! Hook falls on the deck. It is very *hard*. Another boy pushes Smee across the deck. But Smee is luckier than the captain. The place he lands on is *soft*.

"Here's Tinker Bell," shouts John. He has rescued her from the ship's cabin. All the Lost Boys cheer as they fight the pirates.

The battle is over at last. Captain Hook is very sore and tired. He soaks his feet in a tub of *hot* water. Smee holds a piece of ice to soothe the captain's poor aching head. It feels nice and *cold*.

"Get me a pillow," the captain moans. A pirate brings a soft pillow for the captain. "Get me a thick slice of cake," the captain roars. Another pirate brings him a thick slice of cake to make him feel better.

Can you find the tallest pirate in the picture? Which one is the shortest?

Everyone is happy because Tinker Bell is safe. The Lost Boys have a party, with all kinds of good things to eat and drink. Peter and John have a make-believe fight. "Here's how we beat the pirates!" shouts Peter.

Two of the boys are hungry. They are eating thick, juicy sandwiches. And some of the boys are thirsty. Do you see them? Who is drinking hot cocoa? Who is drinking cold lemonade?

Some of the boys sit on the bed and on soft pillows. Which ones are sitting on something hard?

After the party Wendy goes for a walk beside the lagoon. "The water is so *smooth*, I can see myself in it," she says. Little fish come to look at the pretty girl at the edge of the lagoon.

Splash! Naughty Tinker Bell swoops down and hits the water. Now the surface is *rough*. Wendy can't see herself anymore. And Tinker Bell has frightened the fish!

"Whee!" the Lost Boys shout. They are having fun sliding down a hill. The slope is grassy and smooth. They slide fast.

"Ouch," groans Cubby. He slides off the grass and onto some rocks. His slide is slow — and rough!

Peter wants to play a trick on the captain. He has three helpers with him.

Which helper is the biggest? Who is the smallest? Which helper is middle-sized?

"Where is that Peter Pan?" Hook wonders. The captain kneels on a smooth, dry rock and looks through his spyglass. But he can't find Peter. Do you know why?

"One, two, three. BOO!" Peter and his helpers scare Captain Hook right into the water. The captain is surprised — and very angry. Does he land on a smooth place, or on a rough place? Is he wet, or is he dry?

"Peter Pan has beaten me this time," thinks Hook. "But some day, I'll catch him."

Now the adventure is over, and Wendy, John, and Michael are home again. "Good-bye, Peter. Good-bye, Tinker Bell." They wave to their friends.

Nana is glad the children are home. Where is she lying? Who is on top of the table?

All night long Wendy, John, and Michael will remember their adventures in Never Land. And all night long they will think about the wonderful things they will do when Peter comes again.

Pleasant dreams!